SYLVIA BROWNE
and CHRIS DUFRESNE

Animals
on the
Other Side

written with Kat Shehata

Illustrated by Jo McElwee

To my beloved grandchildren, Angelia, William, and Jeffrey whom I cherish. —*Sylvia C. Browne*

To my wonderful children, Angelia and William, who hold my heart. —*Chris Dufresne*

To my husband, Ash, my girls, Ali and Chrissy, my son Andrew, and to Jo Jo. —*Kat Shehata*

To my family, Kat, Aaron and Dana, and to all my precious grandchildren. —*Jo McElwee*

Special thanks to Linda Rossi.

Text copyright © 2005 Sylvia Browne and Chris Dufresne
Illustrations copyright © 2005 Jo McElwee
All rights reserved

First U.S. edition 2005
printed in China

Browne, Sylvia.
    Animals on the other side / by Sylvia Browne and her son, Christopher Dufresne with Kat Shehata ; illustrated by Jo McElwee.
    p. cm.
    SUMMARY: Explanation and consideration of what animals experience in the afterlife and the concept of good and bad as they apply to animals' nature.
    Audience: Ages 8-12.
    ISBN 0-9717843-4-5

    1. Future life--Juvenile literature. 2. Animals--Miscellanea--Juvenile literature. 3. Human-animal communication--Juvenile literature. [1. Future life.
2. Animals--Miscellanea. 3. Human-animal communication.]
I. Dufresne, Chris. II. Shehata, Kat. III. McElwee, Jo.
IV. Title.

BF1999.B76 2005   133.9'01'3
                                      QBI04-700443

ANGEL BEA PUBLISHING

www.angelbea.com
Cincinnati, Ohio

"For most of us, in this lifetime or any other, the most difficult moments of our lives stem from the loss of a family member. If you are an animal lover like me, the loss of a beloved pet is as devastating as the loss of a person.

Let me tell you, without a shadow of doubt, our pets will be waiting for us on the Other Side."

—Sylvia C. Browne

"All the pets I have had throughout my life are still with me to this day. The spirit of my dog Lance, a German Shepherd, is always with our family.

Although he died many years ago, he is still around playing and watching over us the way he always did. All of our other pets see him, too, and play with him just as if he never left."

—Chris Dufresne

When Jolie's body died, her spirit went Home.

I loved my dog, Jolie, with all my heart. As an animal lover, you can imagine the pain I felt when the vet told me Jolie was not going to live. She had congestive heart failure and the doctor suggested we put her down. I couldn't bear the thought. I held Jolie as she lay dying in my arms. At the moment of her passing, I saw a magnificent swirl of white light. I closed my eyes and immediately saw Jolie running (not walking) through the tunnel that leads to the Other Side. I had literally witnessed my dog going Home.

Her friends, Lance and Buddy, were waiting to greet her.

I want all of you to know, without a glimmer of uncertainty, that all of our pets, and animals of every kind, live on the Other Side, also known as "heaven" or "the afterlife." Anyone who has ever been around an animal for more than five minutes can see that God's amazing creatures have minds of their own, unique personalities, and, of course, souls. It goes without saying then, that when an animal dies, its soul goes Home just like ours.

She frolicked with them in the gardens, jumping, barking, and playing.

When people die, they see a tunnel in front of them that leads to the Other Side. Some go straight through, some hesitate as if they are thinking about it for a moment, while still others decide not to go through the tunnel and thus remain earthbound as ghosts. Animals, on the other hand, do not hesitate at all. The second the tunnel is opened for them they burst right through and enjoy the immediate company of their family members and eternal friends.

Then she dashed through the wild jungles of South America,

Animals know exactly where they are going before they pass. During their life on earth they go Home to visit while their bodies are resting. Home is very familiar to animals and that is why there are no animal ghosts. Ghosts are spirits that, for varying reasons, choose not to go through the tunnel that leads to eternal happiness on the Other Side. Many times people tell me they see animal spirits or hear them barking, meowing, or tromping through their house. These animals are not ghosts, but it is not just your imagination either. Animals *are* here on earth from the Other Side.

Splashed in the water along the shores of Atlantis,

There are animals here from the Other Side to watch over and protect us. These animals are called *totems*. Our totems are any of the various creatures of the animal kingdom we have chosen to stand watch at our side to protect us. My totem is an elephant and Chris' is a Grizzly bear. In addition to totems, our pets also visit us from the Other Side. You are not crazy if you feel the spirit of your cat rubbing against your legs, hear the sound of your old dog's toenails clicking on the wood floor, or hear the familiar song your bird used to sing every day before she passed. Our pets do come back to visit us and to remind us that they are still very much alive. And yes, they can hear us when we talk to them just as all of our loved ones who have passed can hear us, too.

Sniffed the magnificent animals of Africa,

Your pets have loved you all through eternity, not just in this lifetime. In fact, the reason they unselfishly chose to come here was to be with you. Animals do not come to earth to learn and experience life like we do. They are perfect just the way God made them. Therefore, there are only two reasons why animals are here on earth. Some of them are here as pets to be with us while we are away from Home. The second reason they are here is to maintain the ecological balance of the earth...the circle of life.

Admired the timeless architecture of Europe,

All God's creatures exist on the Other Side with only one exception. The only living things I have never seen at Home are insects. I am not sure exactly why that is, but I have never seen a spider, mosquito, fly, or any other type of insect. Maybe this exception is just unique to me because I do not particularly care for bugs. If you are a bug lover maybe there will be plenty of them there for you!

Played chase around the splendid palaces of Asia,

That leads me to a question I am frequently asked: "What does the Other Side look like?" The Other Side looks just like the earth in its natural, unpolluted, unspoiled beauty. There are hills and mountains, lakes, trees, oceans, and flowers spread throughout nine continents. There are the seven continents we recognize on earth plus two lost continents, Atlantis and LeMuria. There are monuments, statues, and magnificent buildings unlike any we have ever seen on earth. There are also familiar landmarks like the pyramids, works of art like Venus de Milo, and natural wonders like the Grand Canyon. Animals that have existed throughout the history of the world are there as well such as dinosaurs, unicorns, griffins, and other species never seen by the human eye.

Pounced in the warm, fluffy snow of Antarctica,

The weather at Home is always a perfect 78 degrees with no rain, storms, hurricanes, tornadoes, or lightning flashes. There are no dark skies, cold winter nights, or extreme heat. There is snow on some continents, but it is not bitter cold or frozen. It is actually warm and fluffy. Flowers, trees, and shrubs grow perfectly and are always in bloom in the gardens. No one at Home is sick, tired, angry, or sad. There are no wars and there is no such thing as pollution. Buildings do exist, such as libraries and meditation centers, and there are countless places of worship, like churches and synagogues. There are also golf courses, tennis courts, swimming pools, dance halls, and sports arenas.

Jumped wild and free in the wilderness of Australia

You might wonder, in the vastness of the Other Side, how you will be able to find your pets when you come Home. Do not give it a second thought! Trust me, your pets will push everyone else aside when you are coming through that tunnel so they can be first in line to greet you. You will not have any trouble recognizing or finding your family members. Your pets will look and act the same on the Other Side as they did here on earth. If your pet was a playful calico cat that liked having her belly rubbed on earth, then she will be the same cat on the Other Side.

Enjoyed the peaceful scenery of LeMuria,

Since all animals exist on the Other Side, it is true that predators and prey live together. Let me explain how this works. At Home, animals as well as people, do not have the same "fight or flight" instincts, nor do they need to hunt or gather food for survival like they do on earth. In other words, all God's creatures exist together without the threat of harm because they no longer have to fight or kill to survive. They live their lives without any worries of having to "eat or be eaten".

And ran with the herds in North America.

With that said let me also explain that there is no such thing as a "bad" animal. On earth animals behave the way God made them. Tigers, snakes, sharks, bears, and wolves, among others, are carnivores. When they kill other animals (or sometimes people) they are doing what they need to do to survive. The fact that they are meat eaters does not make them bad. This is the circle of life that God created for us on earth. It is necessary to keep the ecological balance of the world.

Jolie stopped running to watch a family reuniting.

On earth and on the Other Side, animals understand what we say when we talk to them. Here, they can understand us, but they are not able to "speak" to us as we do to them. Of course they do communicate by wagging their tails, purring, braying, or resting their heads in our lap or on our shoulder as a sign of affection. On the Other Side we can communicate with animals telepathically. That means we will clearly be able to exchange our thoughts with each other without even opening our mouths.

She is anxiously waiting to greet her family when they come Home.

The Other Side is a place of beauty, tran-
quility, and perfect harmony. Rest assured
that God loves the animals He created, just
as He loves us. The Other Side would not
be Home without our loyal, unselfish,
beloved animals. Our pets have been and
will be with us for all eternity. Every animal God created will go Home when its
life on earth is over. Not only are they
anxiously waiting to see us again, but they
will be the first ones to greet us when we
arrive Home.

Sylvia and Chris support the following organizations

They are devoted companions who give us their unconditional love and acceptance. For a pet caregiver, the loss of an animal friend can be one of life's most difficult experiences.

Making a donation to the HSUS is a personal way to honor the memory of a pet or person-a kindred spirit. This meaningful gesture will keep the spirit of a lost loved one alive, while helping all animals.

The HSUS will send a card of sympathy to the person or family you designate, acknowledging your thoughtful donation.

For more information about the Humane Society's *Kindred Spirits Memorial Program* visit **www.hsus.org/kindred**

THE MONTEL WILLIAMS MS FOUNDATION

Founded in 2000, the year after Montel Williams was diagnosed with the disease, **The Montel Williams MS Foundation** is dedicated to furthering the scientific study of multiple sclerosis. Its goals are to provide financial assistance to select organizations and institutions conducting the most current research, to increase allocations for research from the federal government and to raise national awareness about MS.

Visit **www.montelms.org** for more information.